Red

Jan De Kinder

Translated by
Laura Watkinson

Eerdmans Books for Young Readers

Grand Rapids, Michigan • Cambridge, U.K.

It's no big deal.

It's something so small. No one else even sees it.

Only me. I point at Tommy's cheeks.

"You're . . . you're blushing . . ."

I wink at Paul.

Paul grins at Freddy.

Lisa bursts out laughing.

We whisper color into Tommy's cheeks.

From tomato to strawberry to cherry red.

"Leave me alone!" says Tommy with a sigh.

But there's no stopping us.

"Do it again! Do it again!" we tell him.

It's like magic.

A snap of the fingers, and his cheeks start glowing.

Tommy's face is as red as a fire truck.

"Leave me alone!" Tommy says again.

Paul laughs.

Every time Paul laughs, Tommy gets a little quieter.

And quieter.

And Paul gets louder.

Much louder.

This isn't funny anymore.

I want it to stop. I want Paul to stop right now.

I actually think Tommy's pretty nice.

But it doesn't stop.

Paul stares at me. "Got something to say?"

He gives Tommy a push.

I shrug my shoulders and bite my lip.

I don't say anything.

I'm scared of Paul.

His tongue is as sharp as a knife.

And his fist is as hard as a brick.

He's twice as strong as me.

There's no way I can stand up to him

on my own.

"Who saw what happened?" our teacher asks.

Should I say something? Why me?

Me? Against the rest of the class?

No way. I'm not crazy.

What I want to do is scream really loud.

And pound my fists.

And yell that it has to stop.

But I stay silent.

"Did anyone see what happened?" the teacher asks again.

You could hear a pin drop.

Paul grins. I gulp.

My mouth won't move, but my hand wants to go up.

No, I don't want to do that.

Not all on my own.

Then Lisa raises her hand.

"I saw it too," she says. Freddy is next.

Then Dan and Lars. Hands in the air.

Everyone saw what happened.

We all talk at once.

I can breathe again.

I'm not all on my own.

It's not over yet.

Paul storms up to me.

"You!" he growls, with his fists up.

Lisa comes to stand beside me. So does Freddy.

"Is there a problem?" says Lisa.

"Got something to say?" asks Freddy.

Paul turns around.

Paul's face has gone green.

Like he's just bitten into a sour apple.

He's not laughing now.

Tommy smiles at me.

"Sometimes I go red," he says.

"Who . . . who doesn't?" I stammer.

"Want to play soccer?" asks Tommy.

I nod. My cheeks are glowing now.

I give the ball a kick.

Jan De Kinder is a children's author and illustrator whose books have been translated into a number of languages. He lives in Belgium. Visit his website at www.jandekinder.be.

For Emma

First published in the United States in 2015 by
Eerdmans Books for Young Readers
an imprint of Wm. B. Eerdmans Publishing Co.
2140 Oak Industrial Dr. NE
Grand Rapids, Michigan 49505
P.O. Box 163, Cambridge CB3 9PU U.K.

www.eerdmans.com/youngreaders

Originally published in Belgium in 2013 under the title
Rood, of Waarom Pesten Niet Grappig Is
by Uitgeverij De Eenhoorn bvba, Vlasstraat 17,
B-8710 Wielsbeke, Belgium

Text and illustrations © 2013 Jan De Kinder
© 2013 Uitgeverij De Eenhoorn bvba
English language translation © 2015 Laura Watkinson

Manufactured at Tien Wah Press in Malaysia

22 21 20 19 18 17 16 15   9 8 7 6 5 4 3 2 1

Library of Congress Cataloging-in-Publication Data

De Kinder, Jan, 1964- author, illustrator.
[Rood, of Waarom pesten niet grappig is. English]
Red / Jan De Kinder.
pages cm
ISBN 978-0-8028-5446-9
[1. Bullying — Fiction. 2. Conduct of life — Fiction.
3. Schools — Fiction.] I. Title.
PZ7.1.D398Red 2015
[E] — dc23
2014031128

The illustrations were created using pencil, charcoal, ink, aquarelle, acrylic, and collage.
The display type was set in Clarendon.
The text type was set in Baskerville.

Flemish Literature Fund

The translation of this book was funded by the Flemish Literature Fund.